KU-143-262

The Railway Rabbits

Fern and the Dancing Hare

Georgie Adams

Illustrated by Anna Currey

Orion
Children's Books

First published in Great Britain in 2011
by Orion Children's Books
a division of the Orion Publishing Group Ltd
Orion House
5 Upper St Martin's Lane
London WC2H 9EA
An Hachette UK Company

1 3 5 7 9 10 8 6 4 2

Printed in Great Britain by Clays Ltd, St. Ives plc.

ISBN 978 1 4440 0158 7

www.orionbooks.co.uk

For Richard and Sandra Ball
New Mills Farm Park, Launceston

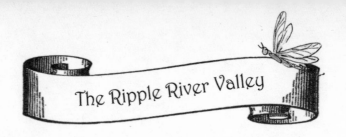

The Ripple River Valley

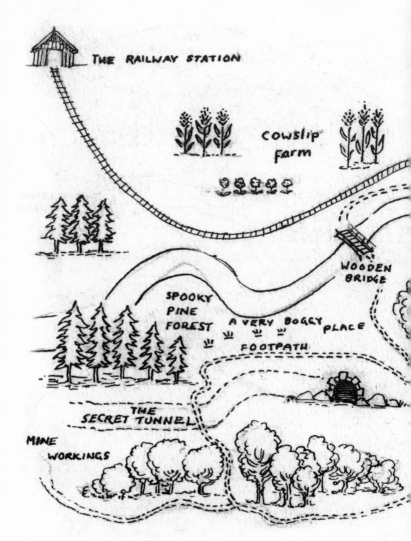

THE RAILWAY STATION

COWSLIP FARM

WOODEN BRIDGE

SPOOKY PINE FOREST

A VERY BOGGY PLACE

FOOTPATH

THE SECRET TUNNEL

MINE WORKINGS

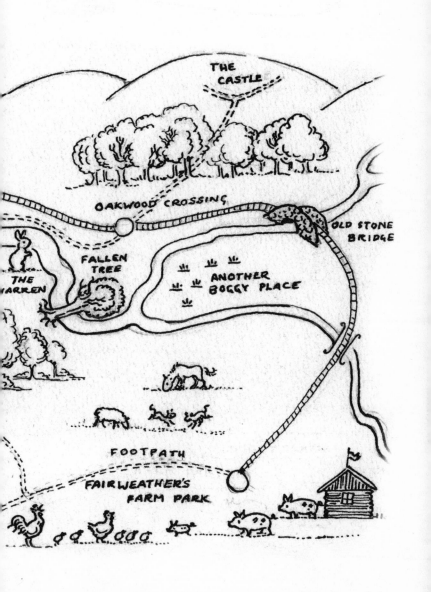

Round and Round in Circles

1

There was great excitement in the
Longears' burrow. Barley was taking
Bramble, Bracken, Berry, Fern and Wisher
to visit his parents for the first time. They
would be spending the night at their
elders' warren. The young rabbits had lots
of questions and were all talking at once.

"What are elders?" asked Fern.

"What are their names?" asked Berry.

"Where do they live?" asked Wisher.

"Is it far?" asked Bramble.

"Where will we sleep?" asked Bracken.

Barley held up his paws. "One at a time!" he said. "Your elders are Marr's parents and mine. Today we're going to see my parents, Blackberry and Primrose Longears. They live at Deep Burrow, under a castle. I grew up there. It's a big warren with plenty of room for us to stay.

We have quite a long journey now I come to think of it. Oh, buttercups! I hope I can remember the way."

"What's a castle?" asked Fern.

"You'll see when we get there," said Barley.

Just then Mellow Longears came hurrying down a tunnel. She was carrying an armful of freshly-picked dandelion leaves.

"You must eat something before you go," said Mellow. To the children she said: "Have you groomed your coats properly and wiped your whiskers? You must look your best for Elderparr Blackberry and Eldermarr Primrose." She peered behind their ears to make sure they were clean.

"Marr!" protested the five young rabbits.

Barley was pacing up and down.

"They look fine," he said. "Come along. We must go."

Fern flung her paws around Mellow's neck.

"I wish you were coming, Marr," she said.

"So do I," said Wisher.

"Another time," said Mellow. "Someone

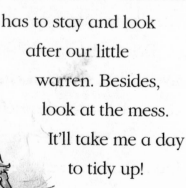

has to stay and look after our little warren. Besides, look at the mess. It'll take me a day to tidy up!

12

Be good and do as Parr tells you.
Remember, only silly rabbits have
careless habits!"

It was a breezy day up-burrow. Playful
puffs of wind ruffled their fur and got
under their tails as Barley and the
young rabbits hopped along. They were
making for a tree, which had fallen over
the River Ripple. It was a good place to
cross the water.

"Race you there," said Bracken.
"Ready. Steady. Go!"

Before Barley could stop them, the
five rabbits set off, racing the short
distance to the tree. He was running to
catch up when he heard a bird calling,
high above his head. Barley froze.

He didn't need to look
up. He knew only one bird
who made that sound. Burdock
the buzzard! Barley thumped his hind
foot quickly on the ground three times.
Thump, thump, thump!

Bramble, Bracken, Berry,
Fern and Wisher felt the
ground shake and stopped. It
was the urgent signal the young rabbits
had been taught to obey from their very

14

first outing up-burrow.
They saw Parr crouching low
in the long grass. Then they
saw the shape of a buzzard's
outspread wings dark against the sky.

"Burdock!" whispered Fern, trembling.

"Down!" Bramble told everyone. "Don't
twitch a whisker."

When Barley looked up, he realised
Burdock was not alone. The buzzard was
flying with his family. The three birds circled

round and round, calling to one another
– *Mew, mew, mew!* Barley was sure it
would be only a matter of time before he
and his young were seen. He watched as
the two big birds flew with slow, heavy
wing-beats upwards then drifted down
on currents of air, while their youngster
flying between them was blown about in
the breeze.

"Ooo!" said Fern, huddling close to
Berry. "We'll all be eaten!"

"It's okay," said Berry. "Look, they're
flying away."

Barley hurried over.

"From now on we must all stay
together," he said. "Who knows what
other dangers lie ahead."

On the other side of the river, they scampered through a tunnel, which ran under the Red Dragon's tracks and came out at Oakwood Crossing. Fern and Berry remembered the last time they were here.

"We were following paw prints in the snow," said Fern. "We were looking for you, Wisher, remember?"

Wisher nodded.

"And I got caught by the Red Dragon!" said Berry.

They all looked around for the monster. There was no sign of him today, but Wisher felt her ears tingle, the way they always did when something was

about to happen. Then she heard a
familiar voice inside her head:

I whisper a song like the wind in your ear.
Wisher, beware. Wisher, take care!

Fern noticed a faraway look in
Wisher's eyes.

"Wait. Listen!" said Wisher.

"I can't see anything," said Bramble.

He stopped. A shrill whistle made
them all jump.

Whooo-Wheeep!

A few minutes later, the Red Dragon
came thundering down the line, spitting

sparks and puffing smoke. The rabbits
shut their eyes and held their breath,
then waited for the worst to happen. But
it never came. The monster rushed by,
hissing clouds of steam.

"Phew!" said Barley. "You were right,
Wisher. Let's go into Oak Wood before the
Dragon comes back."

Barley was confused. It had been a while
since he had last been in Oak Wood.
Tracks and trails he'd once known so
well looked different, or had disappeared
under tangled growth. The trees looked
bigger too. Everything seemed to have
changed. After he had led the young
rabbits round in circles for some time,
Barley stopped at a place where two

paths met. He
tugged his
ear, trying to
decide which
way to go.

"We're lost!"
said Bracken.

"I'm afraid
we are,"
admitted
Barley.

He was beginning to think they'd
never find their way out of the wood
when Fern gave a shout.

"Look," she said. "Paw prints!" She
pointed along one of the pathways. "They
look like the ones Berry and I tracked in
the snow. I'm sure those belong to Blinker
Badger."

"Let's follow them, Parr," said Berry.

"If we find Blinker, we'll ask for
his help."

Sure enough, the tracks led straight
to Blinker's sett. They found the badger
outside, playing with his cubs.

"Barley Longears!" Blinker cried,
patting his old friend on the back. "What
brings you here?"

Barley explained. "And we, er, took one or two wrong turnings before Fern spotted your tracks. I need your help, Blinker," he finished.

Blinker chuckled. It wasn't the first time he'd helped the Longears family. Not so long ago he'd joined a search party to look for Berry.

"Getting lost is becoming a habit, Barley," he said with a twinkle in his eye.

Then he set them on the right path for Deep Burrow.

The Sky Monster

2

"What's that?" said Fern, pointing to the top of a hill.

"The castle," said Barley. "It was built by people-folk a long time ago. Deep Burrow lies beneath its walls."

The Longears had come out of Oak Wood and were standing at the bottom of the hill. The way ahead was steep and there weren't many places to hide. Barley was surprised to see lots of people-folk walking and playing near the castle.

He couldn't remember there being so
many when he was a young rabbit.
There was something else too. His nose
twitched. The breeze blew an unwelcome
smell to his nose. It told him there were
dogs! Barley couldn't see them, but he
warned Bramble, Bracken, Berry, Fern
and Wisher to be careful.

"I'm not afraid of silly old dogs," said
Bramble, sounding braver than he felt.

"They won't catch me," said Bracken.
"I can run fast."

"If I see one, I'll pull his tail!" said
Berry.

Fern gave her brothers a look.

"Dogs are dangerous," she said.

The bucks rolled their eyes.

"We know that," said Bramble and Bracken.

"We were only joking," said Berry.

"Dogs aren't funny," said Fern.

"No, they're not," said Wisher.

"The point is," said Barley quickly, "we must all be very careful. Stay close. And no running off!"

They made their way slowly up the hill, stopping every now and then to see if it was safe to go on. Near the top, they spotted one dog running around. Luckily it was chasing after a stick and didn't notice the rabbits.

"Are we nearly there?" said Wisher.

"Almost," said Barley, keeping one eye on the dog. With the other he caught sight of his parents, waiting for them outside Deep Burrow.

"Look! There's Eldermarr and Elderparr. They're waving. Follow me."

What came next happened so fast, it took them all by surprise. A grinning monster swooped from the sky, soared into the air and dived again. Barley couldn't believe his eyes. He'd never seen anything like it.

The rabbits
froze. The sky
monster flew up,
danced about in the
wind, then plunged again
with frightening speed. Again
and again.

Crouching with the others,
Bracken looked towards Deep
Burrow. It wasn't far. He was sure
he could outrun the beast and dash
to safety.

"I'm off!" he said, and he was gone.
Bracken was quick, but not quick enough.
The crazy creature suddenly crashed to
the ground, and Bracken got caught in its
tail! He lay still for a minute, not daring to
move. When he tried to get up, he found
he couldn't. The stringy tail had wound
itself around his legs.

"Oh no," said Bracken. "I should have stayed with Parr."

Barley, Bramble, Berry, Fern and Wisher watched in horror. Just when it seemed things couldn't be worse, the dog dropped its stick and bounded across the grass towards Bracken.

"Quick!" said Barley. "We must do something."

When they reached Bracken, he was kicking and wriggling to get free. He had seen the dog too.

"Keep still," said Wisher. "We'll soon have you out of this mess."

Wisher and Fern struggled to untie the tail with their paws, while Barley, Bramble and Berry kept a lookout. The dog was fast approaching, yapping noisily.

"It's no good!" said Fern. "The tail is too tight."

"I've got an idea," said Wisher.

She took the tail in her teeth and bit through it. With a couple of kicks, Bracken sprang to his feet.

By now the elders were calling to them.

"Run, run!" shouted Blackberry.

"Over here!" cried Primrose. "Come on. You can do it!"

Barley, Bramble, Bracken, Berry, Fern

and Wisher ran like the wind, the dog barking and snapping at their heels. Just in time, they reached the castle walls, and one by one dived headlong into the burrow.

Deep
Burrow
3

Barley and the five young rabbits
followed Blackberry and Primrose down
a tunnel. The elders were anxious to get
everybody safely into Deep Burrow. They
could still hear the dog barking furiously
at the entrance.

"Goodness," said Primrose, as they
hopped round a corner. "He sounds
fierce!"

They went further and further inside
the warren. Soon only the pit-pit-patter

of their feet could be heard as they ran along one passageway after another. In places, smaller tunnels branched off. The five young rabbits were amazed. The warren was huge! Several times they had to scramble over crumbling walls, buried deep underground.

On either side of a wider corridor they passed hollows full of food, neatly stacked and stored – corn cobs, hazelnuts, brambleberries and much more.

They saw some mice, nibbling at
the stores.

"Who are they?" asked Fern, as they
turned sharply right and went down
a slope.

"We share our home with a family
of mice," said Blackberry. "There are so
many, I'm afraid I don't know them all!
But they are welcome. We have plenty of
room and food to spare."

From the maze of dark passages, they
came suddenly into a large, wide cavern.

The roof and walls were a mass of twisted tree roots. The light was dim, but they could see they were in a very big place.

"Welcome to Deep Burrow!" said Blackberry. "Now, Barley Longears, let me have a good look at your family. Gather round everybody and tell me your names."

The young rabbits introduced themselves:

"I'm Bramble."

"I'm Bracken."

"I'm Berry."

"I'm Fern."

"And I'm Wisher!"

Fern thought Blackberry looked just like her parr with his black and white fur and unusually long ears, and she told him so.

"Let me see," said Blackberry, looking a bit puzzled. He scratched one ear. "You're . . . Wisher?"

Primrose shook her head and smiled. She had soft, grey fur and twinkling eyes.

"Don't be silly, Blackberry," she said. "This is Fern. Look. She has a grey coat, like mine, and wisps between her ears. Wisher has silvery fur. She's the smallest."

"I always get names in a muddle," said Blackberry.

"I'll help you," said Primrose. "Bramble has a shiny black coat, like yours. Bracken is gingery-brown. Berry is easy to remember. He's as red as a holly berry! And Barley..."

"I can remember *his* name," said Blackberry.

Barley laughed.

"I should hope so," he said. "I'm your son!"

It had been some time since Barley had seen his parr. While they talked about this and that, Primrose showed the young rabbits some interesting things. In the middle of the floor stood a stone pillar. It was chipped and broken in places.

"What's that, Eldermarr?" asked Fern.

"It was once part of the castle," said Primrose.

"What is a castle?" asked Fern.

"It's where important people-folk used to live," said Primrose. "There was a king here once. He was a ruler of people-folk, you see? But that was many moons ago."

Around the base of the pillar, Fern noticed a carving. At first she thought it was a circle of rabbits. When she took a closer look she wasn't so sure. Her parr had long ears, but not as long as these animals.

37

"What are those?" she asked.

"Hares," said Primrose. "Dancing hares."

Wisher was staring at the carving too. She had one of her dreamy looks.

"They're moving," said Wisher quietly. "The hares are dancing round and round."

Bramble, Bracken and Berry came over and peered at them.

"They look as still as stones to me," said Bramble.

"Wisher can be a bit strange," said Bracken.

"She sometimes sees things before they happen," said Berry. "Like today. Wisher knew the Red Dragon was coming before we did."

Primrose pricked her ears.

"How interesting," she said. She turned to Wisher and smiled. "You have a wonderful gift. Your great-great-eldermarr, Meadow Silvercoat, had special powers too. Perhaps she has passed them on to you?"

Wisher's pink ears turned pinker still. She didn't understand why she should be the only one to see and hear things. She didn't feel special. She just was.

39

Fern came to her rescue by asking more about the hares.

"There's a story about a dancing hare called Harker," said Primrose. She promised to tell them about him at bedtime.

The young rabbits had fun exploring the rest of the cavern. Fern couldn't stop thinking about Harker the dancing hare. She was looking forward to hearing his story later. As she hopped about she noticed lots of beautiful and unusual objects, tucked into nooks and crannies around the walls. Some things were familiar, but others were strange.

Among the treasures she found:

a bird's egg,

some mossy twigs,

two buttons,

three acorn cups,

a hairclip bow,

a four-leafed clover,

six old coins,

some pretty stones

and

a butterfly wing.

Primrose was delighted to see Fern taking an interest in her collection and explained what everything was.

"I love finding pretty shiny things," said Primrose. "I'm like a magpie!"

Then Blackberry came in banging a tin can with a stick.

CLANG, CLANG, CLANG!

"Time to go up-burrow," he said. "I have a surprise."

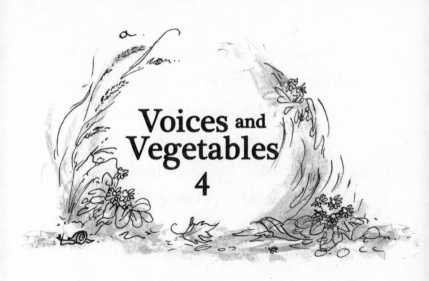

Voices and Vegetables
4

Blackberry led the young rabbits along a short passage. It was different to the way they'd come before. After scrambling up a slope they came to a flight of twisty, stone steps. They hopped up one step at a time, round and round. Near the top they could see daylight through an archway. Bracken stopped and twitched his ears.

"I hope the sky monster and that dog aren't about," he said.

"Don't worry," said Blackberry. "You find dogs and sky monsters where there are people-folk. Humans aren't allowed where we're going. It's too dangerous!"

Feeling much happier, everyone followed Blackberry outside. They were inside the castle walls – or what was left of them. Some parts were loose or had fallen away. In the middle was a mound, overgrown with weeds and grass. The rabbits hopped to the top, then down the other side. Fern looked around. She couldn't see anything dangerous.

"Why aren't people-folk allowed here?" she said. "It looks all right to me."

"Come with me. I'll show you," said Blackberry.

Fern, Wisher, Bramble, Bracken and Berry followed Blackberry across a courtyard of cracked and broken slabs to a cold, shady corner.

"There," he said, pointing to a big hole in the ground. It was covered with iron bars. The young rabbits peered into the gloom.

"It's just a hole," said Bramble. "What's dangerous about a silly old hole?"

His voice echoed back.

Hole - hole – hole – hole – hole!

Bramble jumped in surprise.

"Ooo!" said Fern. "It must be a very deep hole. I can't see the bottom."

"It is a bit scary," said Bracken.

"For a hole," agreed Berry.

Wisher didn't say anything. Her ears started to tingle.

"There's a dungeon down there," said Blackberry.

"What's a DUN-GE-ON?" asked Bramble.

"It's a place where people-folk were kept," said Blackberry. "If someone did something bad, that's where they'd put them."

"But why is it dangerous?" asked Fern.

"Well," said Blackberry. "If anyone fell in, they'd never get out! Besides, a nasty big rat lives down there. I'd never dare go inside the dungeon myself."

Wisher leaned forward with her head right through the bars. She thought

she could hear strange voices floating up
from the depths:

Wisher, beware. Wisher, take care!
The lost . . .

"Wisher!" shouted Fern, pulling her
back. "You could have fallen in. You'd be
down there for EVER!"

"Or be eaten by the rat," said Berry.

"Oh, Fern!" said Wisher. "I heard
voices. I think they were trying to tell me
something important."

"You and your voices," said Bramble.
"We all heard one just now. It was me!"

"No," said Wisher. "These were
different."

"Whatever they were," said Blackberry, "Fern is right, Wisher. You could have fallen through the bars. Come along, everybody. I have something much more exciting to show you."

On the far side of the courtyard beneath an archway was a small wooden gate. Blackberry squeezed under it, quickly followed by Bramble, Bracken, Berry, Fern and Wisher.

What the young rabbits saw next made them gasp. They were in a garden with rows and rows of delicious-looking vegetables and fruit trees. Wonderful smells filled the air and their noses twitched with excitement.

"There!" said Blackberry. "My vegetable garden. Well, it's not mine exactly. The people-folk grow things. When they're not around, I help myself. I'm sure they don't mind. There's plenty for everyone."

"Bugs and beetles!" said Fern. "I've never seen so much food!"

"We usually eat grass," said Bramble.

"Dandelion leaves," said Bracken.

"Anything we can find," said Berry.

"I wish we had a garden like this," said Wisher.

"We must gather food for later," said Blackberry.

They hopped up and down the rows, picking this and nibbling that. Berry saw some round, red fruit hanging from a vine.

"What are these?" he asked, tugging at the biggest one with his paws. *Squish! Squash!* Juice squirted out and dribbled down his cheeks.

Berry looked so funny the others couldn't help laughing.

"It's called a tomato," said Blackberry. "A very ripe one!"

There were many new things to try. Blackberry named them all as they went along.

They picked:

carrots,

cabbage,

radishes,

beans,

strawberries,

and lots of lettuce!

Then they went home with as much as
they could carry.

The Story of Harker Hare 5

That evening Blackberry, Primrose, Barley and the five young rabbits enjoyed a fine feast. They ate until their tummies were full. Afterwards Blackberry told everyone more about Deep Burrow.

"There have been Longears living here for many years," he said. "It all began with your great-great-elderparr, Barleycorn Longears. When he married your great-great-eldermarr, Meadow Silvercoat, they thought it would be a fine place to bring up their children, you see?"

Bramble, Bracken, Berry, Fern and Wisher nodded, trying to take it all in.

"Barleycorn Longears dug this warren with his own paws," said Blackberry.

"There have been Longears living here ever since."

"I was born here," said Barley. "I had seven brothers and sisters to play with."

"Yes," said Primrose. "I seem to remember you were the naughtiest one, Barley. You were always running off on your own!"

"Me?" said Barley.

The young rabbits looked at him, wide-eyed with disbelief.

"Parr!" they protested. "You're always telling us not to do that."

"And he's quite right!" said Primrose.

Then it was time for bed.

THE LONGEARS / SILVERCOAT FAMILIES

BARLEYCORN LONGEARS
OF DEEP BURROW
GREAT - GREAT - ELDER PARR

|

BUTTERWORT LONGEARS
& POPPY
GREAT - ELDER PARR
& GREAT - ELDER MARR
LONGEARS

|

BLACKBERRY LONGEARS
& PRIMROSE
ELDER PARR *&* ELDER MARR
LONGEARS

MEADOW SILVERCOAT
OF CASTLE HILL
AND GREAT - GREAT - ELDER MARR

|

WOODRUFF SILVERCOAT
& MALLOW
GREAT - ELDER PARR
& GREAT - ELDER MARR
SILVERCOAT

|

EYEBRIGHT SILVERCOAT
& WILLOW
ELDER PARR *&* ELDER MARR
SILVERCOAT

BARLEY LONGEARS AND MELLOW SILVERCOAT
PARR AND MARR

BRAMBLE   BRACKEN   BERRY   FERN   WISHER
BUCK   BUCK   BUCK   DOE   DOE

57

"I'm sleeping here," said Bracken.

"I found it first." said Bramble.

"This one's mine," said Berry.

The bucks were jumping in and out of hollows, trying to decide where to sleep. There were so many places to choose from! It was the first time any of the young rabbits had slept away from home. Fern didn't want to sleep on her own in a strange place.

"You can share with me," said Wisher. "This one's big enough for us both."

When Primrose came to say goodnight, Fern reminded her to tell them the story about Harker the dancing hare.

"Oh," said Primrose. "I almost forgot. Gather round everyone. I shall sing you a song:

Long, long ago, in days gone by,
A hare danced on the hill.
And, quite by chance, he
caught the eye
Of Princess Daffodil.

The princess loved to watch
him play;
She called him Harker Hare.
And Harker hopped up every day,
To dance before her there.

Then, one day, poor Harker died,
He lay upon the hill.
The little princess cried and cried
To find him quiet and still.

The story goes, some say it's true,
Her tears like raindrops fell.
And from these drops,
a river grew –
The one we know so well.

The River Ripple is its name,
Long may it gently flow.
So let us thank the hare who came
And danced so long ago.

"It's a sad song," said Wisher, when Primrose had finished.

"It's been passed from rabbit to rabbit, since the days of Barleycorn Longears," said Primrose. "Your great-great-elderparr knew all about Harker and how the river was made."

"Is it a true?" asked Fern. "Was the river really made from tears?"

"It's believed to be true," said Primrose. "But there's another part to the story. A mystery!"

"Ooo!" said the rabbits.

They wriggled their bottoms to sit more comfortably, and Primrose continued.

"When Harker died, the princess was very sad. Her father, the king, wondered what he could do to cheer her up. He gave his daughter a necklace, hung with a tiny silver hare. It was an exact likeness of Harker. The princess was delighted and wore her necklace everywhere. Then, one day, when she was playing in the garden, the necklace snapped and the hare rolled away. The castle grounds were searched, but the silver hare was never found.

In time, the king ordered his craftsmen to carve dancing hares around a pillar. He said it would always remind them of Harker."

"Is that what we saw today?" asked Fern.

"Yes," said Primrose. "The carving has lasted all this time. People-folk believed dancing hares brought good luck. Barleycorn Longears thought the silver hare was lucky too. He said it would bring luck to anyone who found it. But to this day, its whereabouts remains a mystery."

Then Primrose kissed them all goodnight.

Bramble, Bracken and Berry raced each other along a passageway to bed.

"Let's look for the silver hare in the morning," said Bramble. "It would be great if we found it."

"Good idea," said Bracken. "I'll come!"

Berry rubbed his eyes. He was very sleepy.

"Me too," he said.

Fern and Wisher snuggled up on a bed of sweet-smelling herbs. For a little while they talked about the lost necklace, until their eyelids began to droop. It had been a long and exciting day and they were soon fast asleep.

A Scary Night
6

Voices woke her. Wisher didn't know how long she had been asleep. Her head was filled with strange images. She'd imagined dancing around the pillar with the hares. Then she'd been up-burrow, holding paws with them in the courtyard. The moon was shining. She could see iron bars, glittering in the moonlight. They were dancing round the big, black hole!

Wisher sat up. The voices were whispering, but she couldn't make

sense of what they were saying. She
remembered hearing the same voices
earlier, when they'd all been up-burrow.
They had been trying to tell her
something. What was it? It came to her
in a flash:

Wisher, take care. Wisher, beware!
The lost . . .

Wisher repeated the last two words
aloud:

"The lost. The lost what?" Her ears
tingled. "It must be a clue. There's only
one thing lost here. The silver hare! I'll go
back to the hole. Maybe the voices will
speak to me again."

Wisher looked across at Fern. She was sound asleep. Should I wake her? thought Wisher. She thought better of it. If I tell Fern where I'm going, she'll say it's dangerous and try to stop me. I must do this on my own. I hope I can find my way.

Wisher crept out of the hollow and ran down a tunnel. After a few wrong turns, she found herself at the foot of the twisty stone steps and went up. At the top, bright moonbeams cast long shadows. The castle ruins looked different at night – some parts in deep shade; others lit by moonlight.

Wisher shivered. She wished she'd asked Fern to come with her. A sudden noise made her jump.

Skreeeeek! Skreeeeek!

It was the screech of an owl! Wisher stayed rooted to the spot. Her heart beat fast. Where was it? Had it seen her? At any moment she expected to feel sharp talons sink into her neck. When she dared to look, Wisher saw the owl swoop low above the courtyard, its wings outstretched. It flew over a wall and disappeared into the darkness.

Wisher waited until she was sure the owl had gone, then she dashed towards the big, black hole.

Fern was woken by a noise.

CHAW, CHAW, CHAW!

The strange sound came to her out of the silence.

CHAW, CHAW, CHAW!

What made noises like that? Rats? She remembered Elderparr Blackberry had said there was a nasty one living in the dungeon. She'd never seen a rat, but Parr had said once: "Never trust a rat. Their teeth are so sharp, they can bite through a barn door!"

CHAW, CHAW, CHAW!

There it was again. Fern listened carefully to the low, regular sound. Is it Wisher snoring? she thought. Yes, that would be it. But when she looked, Wisher wasn't there.

Fern began to panic. Something awful must have happened. Had a horrid rat snatched her while she was sleeping? It might be eating her at this very minute!

CHAW, CHAW, CHAW!

She had to do something.

Fern's heart raced as she ran along a tunnel. Every now and then she stopped, trying to decide where the noise was coming from.

There were so many passages it was hard to tell. After a while she turned down a wider passage. Fern wrinkled her nose. The air smelled sweeter.

The tunnel went on straight for a short way, then dipped suddenly down before a bend. Beyond that she could see a glow of light. The sound grew louder.

Fern dreaded what might be around the corner. But there was no turning back. She kept close to the wall, her feet hardly making a sound.

Pit-pat-patter-pat. She trod on something hard. At first Fern thought it was a stone. Then she saw it was a small, round nut. Further on there was another, and another – a trail of half-eaten hazelnuts!

Fern followed the nut trail. A few hops ahead, part of the roof had fallen in. Now she could see where the light was coming from.

Through an opening, a beam of moonlight shone into the tunnel. A little further on something big was blocking her way. What Fern saw next, stopped her in her tracks.

Two big ears.

A pointed nose.

Sharp teeth.

Fern looked about for a place to hide.
There were no nooks or crannies here,
only solid walls. To her horror the monster
stepped out of the shadows into the
moonlight.

It was a mouse.

"Phew!" said Fern. "I thought you were a rat."

"You gave me a fright too," squeaked the mouse. "I thought YOU were a rat!"

They laughed.

"I'm Trip," said the mouse.

"I'm Fern Longears," said Fern. "Was it you making that noise?"

"Probably," said Trip. "Well, not just me. Let me introduce my family." Behind him more mice peeped out from a pile of nuts. "It's all right. Fern's a friend."

The mice scampered from their hiding places and ran about squeaking. Fern remembered seeing mice in the food stores when they'd first arrived. She asked if they were family too.

"Yes," said Trip. "Blackberry and Primrose Longears are very kind. They let us help ourselves to food."

Fern noticed a large block of wood, barring their way. A hole had been gnawed through the bottom. She could see teeth marks. It jolted her memory. Rats! Sharp teeth! In a flash Fern remembered why she had come. She'd been thinking about rats when she'd discovered Wisher was missing.

"Wisher!" she said. "I'm looking for my sister. She's a small rabbit with silvery fur."

The mice shook their heads.

"Oh!" said Fern. "I'm afraid something awful has happened to her. I must go back and tell Parr. But I don't know the way."

"We'll help you," said Trip. "We can take a shortcut through this door." He pointed to the hole at the bottom of the thick, wooden block.

"What's in there?" asked Fern.

"A dungeon," said Trip.

Fern gasped. What had Elderparr Blackberry said about the dungeon?

A nasty rat lived in there! But she had no choice, so she followed the mice through the hole.

Down in the Dungeon 7

Trip led the way down steep stone steps to the dungeon floor. Fern's nose twitched. It smelled damp in this dark and gloomy place. She imagined rats hiding in the deep shadows, waiting to pounce.

"How do we get out?" she asked Trip, as they hurried along a wall. As far as Fern could tell, the wall looked solid.

"There's a gap in the corner," said Trip. "Not far now. It leads to a passage near the stores. From there it's a short run back to where you started. Don't worry, I never get lost. I know Deep Burrow like the back of my paws!"

As Fern and Trip reached the gap, a moonbeam shone through an opening above their heads. A movement made Fern look up. There was a rabbit peering down through some bars at the top. It was a small, silvery-white rabbit.

"Wisher!" cried Fern.

Wisher was amazed to see Fern too.

"What are you doing?" she said.

"Looking for you!" said Fern crossly.

"I thought something had happened."

"Something
has happened,"
said Wisher excitedly. "I
heard voices and". . .

"Wisher, not now," said
Fern. "These mice are showing
me the way out of the dungeon." She
turned to Trip. "Come on. Let's go!"

"No, wait," said Wisher urgently.
"Listen. Please listen! It's about the hare."

Wisher, take care. Wisher, beware!
The lost silver hare is somewhere
down there.

Fern's eyes opened wide in surprise.

"Bugs and beetles!" she said. "The hare is in the dungeon!"

Trip and the mice chattered among themselves at this exciting news. They'd heard about the lost hare too.

"It could be anywhere," said Fern, looking nervously about. "I'm sure I can smell a rat."

"Be careful," said Wisher. "I can't come down. It's too far too jump."

"We'll help," said Trip. "Ten pairs of eyes are better than one."

"Thank you," said Fern. "Go back to the others, Wisher. I'll see you soon, I promise."

"Good luck!" said Wisher.

Then she was gone.

Fern and the mice searched the dungeon. Trip and his family ran about squeaking and falling over one another's tails. They had turned Hunt the Hare into a game! Soon the first rays of the morning sun shone down on them.

Fern was beginning to think it was a hopeless task. They had looked everywhere, but there was still no sign of the hare.

"Maybe the voices were wrong after all," she told Trip, feeling very disappointed.

The mice sat down. Even they had

grown tired of playing. Just then a golden sunbeam pierced the gloom, and a shiny object caught Fern's eye.

There, on the dungeon floor

Something bright.

Something silvery . . .

"Look, Trip," said Fern, hardly able to speak. "Your paws are smaller than mine. Can you see what it is?"

Trip reached down. From a crack in the floor, he pulled a tiny silver hare.

"Oh," said Fern, taking it in her paw. She held the hare up for the mice to see. "I've found it. I've found the lucky hare!"

Trip and the mice danced round and round.

"Hooray!" they shouted. "Hooray!"

Dancing Home
8

At dawn, the Longears gathered to celebrate. Trip and the mice were invited to join the rabbits on this special occasion. Everyone was talking at once.

"Oh, my ears and whiskers!" said Primrose, holding up the silver hare. "Well done, Fern!"

"I couldn't have found it without Wisher," said Fern. "She told me where to look."

"It was the voices," said Wisher.

"We helped," said Trip.

"You were lucky you didn't meet a rat," said Blackberry. "There's a nasty, big one in the dungeon."

"Very lucky!" agreed Barley.

"Fern was very brave," said Berry.

"I wish I'd found the hare," said Bramble.

"So do I," said Bracken.

They talked their tails off!

Primrose gave the hare back to Fern.

"You found it. You must keep it,"
she said.

Fern shook her head.

"It belongs at Deep Burrow, Eldermarr,"
she said. "Harker danced on the hill. I'd
like it to stay here."

"Thank you, Fern! The silver hare
shall be the pride of my collection." said
Primrose. "Now, we must find the right
place to put it. You choose."

Fern knew just where it should go. She
gently placed the silver hare beside the
butterfly wing.

"It will remain here for everyone to enjoy," said Blackberry. "For many years to come."

"For you, and some day, your children," said Primrose to the five young rabbits.

"For as long as there are Longears at Deep Burrow!" said Barley.

Something made Fern glance at the carving around the base of the pillar. She couldn't be sure, but she thought she saw the hares moving. Wisher saw them too. She knew there was no doubt about it. The hares were dancing for joy.

After promising to come
again soon, Barley and
the children set off for
home. The young rabbits

happily hopped, skipped and rolled down
the hill as the sun rose over the castle.
It was too early for people-folk. There
wasn't a dog or a sky monster in sight!

When they entered Oak Wood, Fern
took the lead. For a reason she couldn't
explain, she felt fearless as she danced
along a path.

"Take care," said Barley. "We
must stay together. Keep your
eyes open for foxes!"

But the only animal they met was Blinker Badger, out walking with his cubs.

"Need any help finding your way home, Barley?" he said.

"Not today, thank you," said Barley. "We're in luck. Fern seems to have found the right path!"

At Oakwood Crossing they hurried through the tunnel. Wisher wondered if the Red Dragon was about, but her ears didn't tingle and there was no sign of him – not even a puff of smoke.

Hopping out on the other side, Barley stopped. He searched the sky for Burdock, but he couldn't see the bird anywhere. Then he saw Fern and the others, way ahead. They were making for the river. Barley caught up with them.

"You're lucky Burdock is hunting elsewhere," he said. "Just remember what your marr always says, 'Only silly rabbits have careless habits!'"

After that they stayed together and ran along the path to the wooden bridge.

Halfway across, Barley, Bramble, Bracken, Berry, Fern and Wisher stopped to look down at the water.

The River Ripple was flowing in a Not-Such-A-Hurry way.

"This river has been here for as long as I can remember," said Barley. "And I hope it always will."

"Eldermarr Primrose said the river was made from tears," said Fern.

"It's a sad story," said Barley. "But it has a happy ending, doesn't it? The river is here for us all to enjoy."

Fern and the others agreed. Then they danced across the bridge, singing:

The River Ripple is its name,

Long may it gently flow.

So let us thank the hare who came

And danced so long ago.

Not far away, Mellow was outside the Longears' warren waiting for their return. She heard them singing and hopped across the meadow to welcome them.

"We've got so much to tell you!"
said Fern.

Visiting Deep Burrow had been quite
an adventure for Barley and the young
rabbits, but it was good to be home!

Acknowledgements

Inspiration for *The Railway Rabbits* came from the view from my window. The Launceston Steam Railway runs along the Kensey river valley, North Cornwall, linking the historic town of Launceston at one end of the line with the hamlet of Newmills at the other. My thanks to Kay and Nigel Bowman for their wonderful railway, Richard and Sandra Ball at New Mills Farm Park – and to all the rabbits in between.

Georgie Adams